ON THIS ISLAND

TRAIL'S END

LARRY KANFER

ON THIS ISLAND

PHOTOGRAPHS OF LONG ISLAND

FOREWORD BY BILL HENDERSON

VIKING STUDIO BOOKS

VIKING STUDIO BOOKS

Published by the Penguin Group

Viking Penguin, a division of Penguin Books USA Inc.,

40 West 23rd Street, New York, New York 10010, U.S.A.

Penguin Books Ltd, 27 Wrights Lane, London W8 5TZ, England

Penguin Books Australia Ltd, Ringwood, Victoria, Australia

Penguin Books Canada Ltd, 2801 John Street, Markham, Ontario, Canada L3R 1B4

Penguin Books (N.Z.) Ltd, 182–190 Wairau Road, Auckland 10, New Zealand

Penguin Books Ltd, Registered Offices: Harmondsworth, Middlesex, England

First published in 1990 by Viking Penguin, a division of Penguin Books USA Inc.

10 9 8 7 6 5 4 3 2 1

Grateful acknowledgment is made for permission to reprint an excerpt from "Look, stranger, on this island now" from *W. H. Auden: Collected Poems* edited by Edward Mendelson. Copyright 1937 and renewed 1965 by W. H. Auden. By permission of Random House, Inc. and Faber and Faber Ltd.

LIBRARY OF CONGRESS CATALOGING IN PUBLICATION DATA

Kanfer, Larry, 1956–

On this island: photographs of Long Island/Larry Kanfer; foreword by Bill Henderson.

p. cm.

"Viking studio books."

ISBN 0-670-83175-1

1. Photography—New York (State)—Long Island—Landscapes.

2. Long Island (N.Y.)—Description and travel—Views.   I. Title.

TR660.5.K35   1990

779′.36′092—dc20   89-40668

Printed in Japan

Set in Fournier

Designed by Fritz Metsch

To Aunt Ethel with my deepest affection

Look, stranger, on this island now

The leaping light for your delight discovers,

Stand stable here

And silent be,

That through the channels of the ear

May wander like a river

The swaying sound of the sea.

—W. H. Auden, "On This Island"

FOREWORD

For several years, while living in Manhattan, I had visited the East End of Long Island in the summer to enjoy its beaches. But one winter I traveled to the North Fork alone, in the middle of January. I happened to walk out onto the shores of Peconic Bay, looking south to Shelter Island, at a moment when the sun, clouds, and water were awesomely matched. Not a boat or a person was in sight. I suddenly thought, "But this is the most beautiful place on earth." Until that moment I had never really seen what I was looking at.

Larry Kanfer's photographs recreate that North Fork moment for me all over again. I now live permanently on the East End and he enables me to see it with a fresh vision.

Kanfer's photographs are celebrations of the delicate balance between sky, beach, water and, now and then, people, too—especially as witnessed through their artifacts. These delicate balances have been shattered in many portions of the Island, especially closer to Manhattan—Brooklyn, Queens, and much of Nassau County. Airline pilots, arriving from the Atlantic, note that the line of smog now begins at Patchogue in Suffolk County and continues well past the New Jersey suburbs to the west.

You will not find smog in these photographs, and honor is not given to asphalt, concrete, and plastic, either. Kanfer chooses what is of enduring value in our landscape—the natural beauty of Long Island that has little to do with people.

Larry Kanfer's previous collection of photographs, *Prairiescapes*, considered the sights of the Midwest. It is no accident that he next turned to Long Island. Much of the land here is flat, like the prairie. The water stretches away from the shore on each side of this 118-mile-long island. As in the Midwest, the sky over it is of great consequence because of the flatness beneath it.

What interests Kanfer is not the great drama of landscape and scene. These photographs are, above all, subtle. He never whaps you over the head with the obvious. He asks you to come to his photographs with him, to participate, and to understand a beauty he himself may also be learning about. In *Prairiescapes* he wrote: "Many times when I recall the process of photographing a particular image, I realize that the meaning of the photograph has changed with the passing of time. Obviously the image itself has not changed, but my perception has been altered to allow for a varying interpretation of the landscape."

A few of these places are immediately recognizable: Ashawagh Hall in

Springs; the waterfront at Sag Harbor; a view of Mulford Farm in East Hampton, with St. Luke's Church in the background. But even these well-known landmarks are captured in a way to give them new meaning.

For instance: Mulford Farm and the church (30). A less inspired photographer might settle for the obvious—a shot from the ancient graveyard across the street. Kanfer captures the colonial houses (circa 1680) in the foreground and the more recently built stone church over their shoulders in the distance. I doubt that anybody who lives out here and looks at the farm and the church every day has contemplated that vision of the old, the newer, and a religious suggestion of the eternal.

But most of these photographs are not as readily placed and part of their fascination is trying to place them. Most of them could be just about anywhere on Long Island, with the exception of portions of Brooklyn, Queens, and Nassau County. I think I have seen all of them, but I am never quite sure where. For instance, the photograph of the tire and dog tracks in the sand and the two boats at mooring in the background is Louse Point (15). I can see Louse Point from my upstairs window. In fact, the paw print in the sand may be that of my Labrador retriever, Sophie, and the sailboat in the distance may very well be my own O'Day daysailer, the *Rotten Reviews*. But this could be a small harbor up-island in Port Jefferson, or a tidal inlet in Orient. Most of these photographs are not only timeless, they are placeless.

Even the photo with a fuzzy view of people through a bar window, "Main Street Tavern" (38), could be Main Street anywhere on Long Island, although it actually belongs to Sag Harbor. Others will nominate different Main Street Taverns. The shot is universal.

The same goes for views of potato fields, elm-shaded lanes, weathered docks, abandoned houses, rusting Agway gasoline pumps, and for many of Kanfer's meditations on the ocean, beach, and sky—placeless, timeless.

Kanfer is correct in selecting water, beach, and sky as his usual subjects, for these are truly a major part of Long Island. This is not only a long place, it is also narrow—about twenty miles at its widest. No matter how we have managed to clutter up the interior of the Island with housing developments, shopping centers, and parking lots, the sea, the bays, and the beaches are always close by. One can flee in minutes from the clutter to the instant solace of sea and Sound only a few miles to the north or south.

Kanfer's exquisite visions remind us finally what it is that we have left of the original Long Island, and how precious it is. As New York City's growth continues its march across Suffolk County (having already captured and transformed the bedroom communities of Nassau County to the west), it threatens the Pine Barrens of Suffolk's Brookhaven Town, the remaining open spaces of the North Fork and also the South Fork, more commonly known as "the Hamptons"—once valued as fertile farmland rather than the showcase of Manhattan professionals showing off their houses to each other across treeless expanses.

These East End towns, on both South and North Forks, are fighting a continuous battle to control development. We who live out here are not unaware of what we are losing year by year and sometimes month by month as bulldozers create roads in the woods and tack up names like Blueberry Hill Walk or Cattle Ramble where one will never find a blueberry or a cow. But despite the determination of organizations like the Nature Conservancy and the Group for the South Fork and many others, we are falling back, literally with our backs to the sea.

Still, as Kanfer's invaluable testament makes evident, there will always be the water, beach, and sky. Although it is rumored that millions of gallons of oil are buried in the Sound and just offshore, I hope that we will never see a nest of oil rigs out there. Perhaps one artifact will remain: our modern cathedral, our Notre Dame and Chartres—the town landfill. Each year, as elsewhere on Long Island, the landfill climbs toward the sky. It is already one of the highest points in East Hampton.

Kanfer takes us back thousands, if not millions, of years to an Island without people. In short, a Long Island that is the opposite of modern Long Island where over seven million humans crowd together.

Before the people came, Long Island was visited by two glaciers. The last one, the Wisconsin Ice Sheet, was hundreds of feet thick and extended across the Island to the ocean. When it began to retreat, about 40,000 years ago, it left behind various boulders and kettle holes such as Lake Ronkonkoma and Lake Success, and the hills of the northern shore. As the ice melted, the water flowed down the ridges toward the ocean, carrying with it the soft parts of the hills. Thus were formed the fertile plains on the Island's south side and the Hempstead Plain, once the largest prairie east of the Mississippi and, as we shall see a bit later in this essay, now something entirely different.

The first humans traveled to Long Island before it was an island, walking across the channel near Manhattan, now called the East River, and passing by a lake that would expand into the Sound. At this time— approximately 13,000 years ago—mastodons still roamed the broad pasture sloping toward an Atlantic Ocean many miles to the south of the present beach. The land was covered with forests, the climate was temperate, the soil was fertile and the sea provided a bounty of fish and shellfish.

Europeans came again to Long Island in 1524, when Giovanni da Verrazano sailed up the Hudson River and turned east, following the Sound coast to what is now Block Island. Verrazano did not land on Long Island, but others were to follow. They discovered about 6,500 Indians on the Island, living in small tribes—thirteen of them—each headed by a sachem. Within a century almost all of them would be wiped out by disease or forced by the new settlers to move to the mainland.

These Indians made few demands on the environment and were at peace both with each other and later with the white visitors. Their major industry was collecting seashells for use as wampum by the more ferocious mainland tribes. They hunted, fished, and farmed. To us, it seems a bit like paradise.

In the seventeenth century, the Europeans settled first on the east end at Gardiner's Island (still in the hands of the original family and as yet relatively unspoiled) and at Southampton and Maidstone (now East Hampton) on the South Fork and at Southold on the North Fork.

On the western end of the Island, Nieuw Amsterdam—soon to become New York—began to grow. From the start the Dutch and the English were fond of Long Island—its climate was similar to what they remembered back home. And there was so much to take here. During the years of the British occupation of New York, in the Revolutionary War, the Island nearby was denuded of wood. The forests were not replanted.

For the next century the land was left in relative peace. Most of the people who settled there thought of themselves as farmers. They grazed their cattle and sheep on the Hempstead Plain and on the South Fork's Shinnecock Hills. They grew corn and fertilized their fields with manure and with the tiny fish known in New England as menhaden.

Soon the settlers discovered another gift from the sea—whales. For years they had whaled close to the shore. Now the hunt for whale ivory and oil sent them to every corner of the globe. The graves of some of these whalers are still to be found in Sag Harbor, which for a time in the midnineteenth century was a major eastern port. By the end of the 1850s, because of the California Gold Rush and the discovery of crude oil in Pennsylvania, the whaling industry was in sharp decline. The last whaling ship departed from Sag Harbor in 1871 and the town was left alone until a recent real estate boom that has resulted in near-gridlock on its main street on summer weekends.

Yet other portions of Long Island were not spared raucous development in the nineteenth century. In 1801, a distant glimmer of that modern horror, the Long Island Expressway, was constructed—the Rockaway Turnpike. The Turnpike was a toll road and made a profit on the New Yorkers who traveled by ferry to Brooklyn Heights and thence to Far Rockaway.

But the real artery of development here as elsewhere in the country was the railroad. Initially, the idea of the railroad was not to convey sweating tourists from New York to the Hamptons or elsewhere, but to take a shortcut through the middle of the Island to Greenport and there make connections for a boat across the Sound to Connecticut and onward to Boston. Long Island was a place to get through and the would-be robber barons expected to make a fortune on the idea.

By 1844 the line did indeed extend all the way from Brooklyn to Greenport. The problem was that it went through vacant land with very few towns along the way. If you didn't want to go to Boston, the line was of no use to you. And it was certainly of no use to the farmers along the way. They were unhappy to see their cows slaughtered by the train and their fields and woods set on fire by the sparks from the wood-burning locomotives. In those days, they took action, ripping up the rails and soaping up the rails at inclines.

Despite these objections, several railroads competed for profit in the rush to develop Long Island. Among them was the Central Railroad, envisioned, financed, and built by A. T. Stewart, mogul of one of the first New York department stores. Stewart's dream was called Garden City. In 1869 he bought nearly 7,000 acres of prairie land on the Hempstead Plain from the town of Hempstead. Anticipating Abraham Levitt's town by many

years, Stewart built a utopian suburban community that he owned—streets, stores, churches, hotel, houses, and railroad station. Nothing was for sale. Everything was for rent.

The trouble was nobody wanted to rent in Mr. Stewart's new town. They wanted to own the houses. After his death in 1876, his widow offered the homes for sale and thus created the modern town of Garden City.

Toward the turn of the century, the Long Island Railroad began determined efforts to lure New Yorkers to the Long Island seaside. The railroad built lines along the south shore and the tourist boom began. The more adventurous tourists explored farther east to the end of the Island. Fashionable hotels were erected on Shelter Island and at Orient Point.

Closer to the city, people with names like Phipps, Morgan, and Whitney were buying land and building on the North Shore where there was plenty of wooded land and a few rolling hills to add character to their estates. They were joined early in the new century by the Vanderbilts, Roosevelts, and Guggenheims on what became known as the Gold Coast. By the outbreak of World War I, 180 estates were strung between Great Neck and Northport, many of them covering over 100 acres.

During the early part of the twentieth century, Long Island became home to the military and to the aircraft industry. In 1927 Charles Lindbergh set out from Roosevelt Field and crossed the Atlantic in thirty-three and a half hours. The history of Roosevelt Field is a microcosm of what would soon happen to the entire Island. In 1936 it was sold to build an automobile racetrack, which eventually turned into Roosevelt Raceway. In 1950 the entire field was sold to a real estate developer who built a shopping center and industrial park on the 400-acre plot. This was one of the earliest shopping centers in America and it is still one of the biggest—the harbinger of hundreds of shopping centers that spread across the Island.

By the end of World War II, shopping centers were a necessity. Fifteen million young men and women were welcomed home with the GI Bill of Rights and entitled to new homes with government-backed mortgages.

Enter Abraham Levitt and sons. Levitt was but one of many developers who looked to Long Island for their visions. The Island's reputation as home to the wealthy was well-remembered from the days of the Roaring Twenties. To much of the country, it seemed the place to be, and Levitt made it even more attractive in 1947 by acquiring a huge parcel on the edge of Hempstead Plain known as Island Trees—an area with no trees at all, and thus easy to develop. He cut Island Trees into sixty-by-one-hundred-foot lots and built over 2,000 houses, which he offered for rent.

But like A. T. Stewart in the previous century, he discovered that nobody wanted to rent his houses; they wanted to own them. Unlike Stewart, Levitt gave in and offered them for sale. Price: $7,500 with a down payment of $500. The houses came in four basic models, with an automatic laundry, a refrigerator, an electric range, and a single sapling in the front yard.

On all of Long Island before the war fewer than 5,000 new houses had been erected per year. By the end of 1951, Levitt had built over 17,400 houses in Levittown. The population of Island Trees went from zero to more than 70,000 in those few years.

The time was ripe for Robert Moses and his parks and parkways. Moses began dreaming about improving Long Island when he was a railroad commuter from Babylon to Manhattan. The long trips made for some profound dreaming—and by 1929 his earliest schemes had resulted in the start of what is now the Southern State Parkway and he had developed Jones Beach on the south shore—complete with a ten-thousand-car parking lot, the biggest in the United States at the time.

It was becoming simple to migrate from Manhattan to Long Island, and even the distant eastern points were easier to reach. Moses oversaw the beginning of the Long Island Expressway, the giant of all Long Island roads. In 1953 it was designed to handle 80,000 cars a day. In a few years it was jammed with 150,000 cars a day, and in modern times they move at a crawl.

Because of the Expressway, the parkways, and the railroad, it is almost all over for rural Long Island. A few farms hold out on the eastern forks, but with land worth more than $150,000 an acre, most farmers have sold to developers. Manhattan has almost completed its march to the east.

As Everett Rattray notes sadly in his classic tribute to the land, *The South Fork*, "They are all gone now; the Indians and the whalers, the Indian whalers, the part-Indians, the part-whalers, the farmer-fishermen, the inheritors of Old Testament tradition and the aboriginal planting lore, the narrow, insular men and women who lived and bred and inbred for two and a half centuries in a backwater-corner of the United States . . ."

Thanks to Larry Kanfer's stunning collection of meditations on the sun, sea, and land, we understand and appreciate an Island that our ancestors knew, but for us is harder to find.

This is not the Island of the tourist. Many of Kanfer's photographs were taken in the off-season, in decidedly unchic weather—mist, fog, rain. It is hard to discover a photograph here that would delight a tourist board . . . baking bodies on a broiling beach, for instance. Kanfer's compositions remind me of my winter moment on the North Fork years ago—an unheralded testament to one of the most stunning places on earth.

Kanfer offers us a revelation of the beauty we can still discover around us, and save, if we only look and try.

Bill Henderson
East Hampton, New York

ON THIS ISLAND

THROUGH A GLASS

WHALING KEEPSAKE

ELM GROVE

To the Sea

LINGERING LEAVES

YACHTS ON OYSTER BAY

COUNTRY STORE

SEA LEVEL

SEASIDE GARDEN

DOCKSIDE

EVENTIDE

ANDREW'S MEADOW

GOLDEN GATES

QUIET COVE

SHARED PATH

DUNE BUGGY ROUTE

WHISPERS OF THE PAST

MORNING IN AMAGANSETT

SAND CASTLES

On Leave

PROMONTORY

VANTAGE POINT

EMPTY NEST

POTATO FIELD

SECRET PASSAGE

SETTLER'S LEGACY

DAWN'S EDGE

AGAWAM PARK MEMORIAL

NATURE'S WAY

EAST HAMPTON TEXTURES

ROSLYN HEIGHTS

AMBER COURTYARD

HALLOWEEN HARVEST

UNDER THE TABLE

AUTUMN'S TEXTURE

COAST GUARD

AUTUMN REPOSE

MAIN STREET TAVERN

SHADED MELON

LAVENDER PORTAL

HALL OF FAME

FARMSTAND

DRY DOCK

AGWAY STATION

SANDY STAIR

SHAKE SHELTER

AT AMAGANSETT

AMBER WAVES

WINDBREAK

SUNRISE AT OYSTER BAY

STORM WARNING

STAIRWAY TO HEAVEN

ROCKWEED

MONTAUK'S LIGHT

SAND TRACKS

SEAWALL

BOATHOUSE

SHORE LEAVE

MIRROR IMAGE

CUNNING COTTAGE

WATERSIDE

FROM THE FERRY

GARDEN OF THE GODS

SOLITUDE

MORNING MARSH

BEACH HOUSE

AFTERNOON SHADOWS

ALL POINTS NORTH

SEA'S EDGE

On the Horizon

SOUTH SHORE SEASCAPE

A Time Forgotten

ASHAWAGH HALL

LOOKOUT

BREAKWATER

ISLANDS IN THE STREAM

ALL ABOARD

BITTERSWEET MEMORY

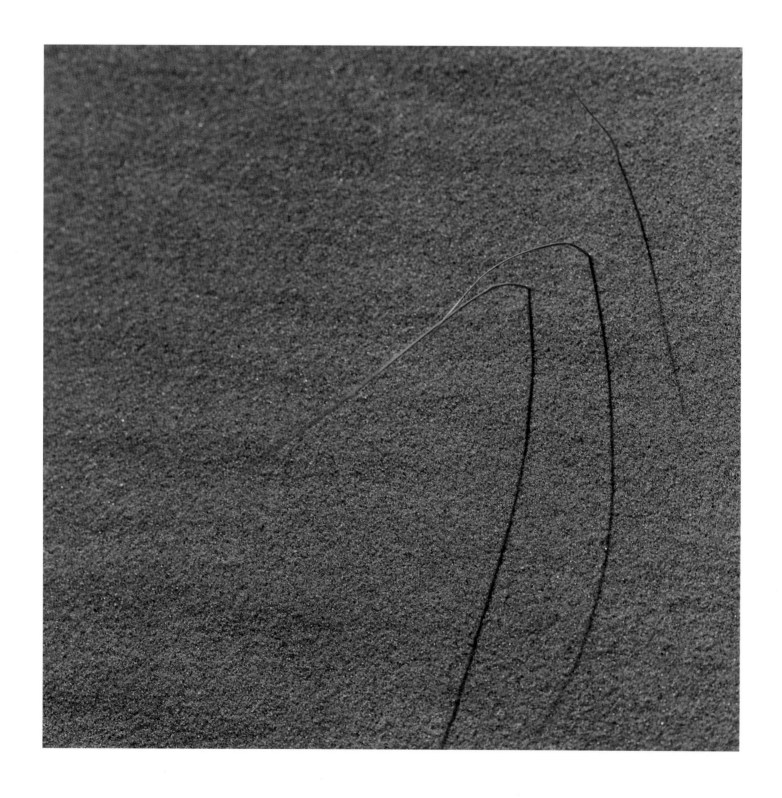

SEA OF SAND

FORBIDDEN VIEW

HOMEGROWN

MIDSEASON BLOOM

GARDEN ENCLOSURE

WINDSWEPT

DRIFTWOOD GARDEN

GRASSY KNOLL

BOARDWALK

OYSTER BAY TRIO

GATEKEEPER'S COTTAGE

ALL IN A ROW

IN A MIST

FINGER SHORE

WEEKEND RETREAT

FADED AFTERNOON

ENDLESS SUMMER

SEAWARD

By the Sea

OYSTER BAY

At the end of the Old Montauk Highway, 1987

1. Montauk Lighthouse, 1988
2. Sag Harbor, 1987
3. At East Hampton, heading north, 1988
4. Near Remsenburg, 1988
5. A quiet lane in Southampton, 1988
6. Oyster Bay, 1988
7. Springs, 1987
8. Montauk Beach, 1988
9. On the Sound, at Montauk Point, 1988
10. Off Ram Island, 1987
11. Looking toward Noyack Bay, 1987
12. Shelter Island, 1987
13. Centre Island, 1988
14. Oyster Bay, 1987
15. Edward Island Sanctuary, 1988
16. Along the South Shore, 1988
17. East Hampton Cemetery, 1988
18. Between Amagansett and the Promised Land, 1988
19. Southampton Beach, 1988
20. Near Ponquogue Point, 1988
21. Off Ram Island Drive, 1987
22. On Accabonac Harbor, 1988
23. At Moneybogue Bay, 1988
24. A view from Alvah's Lane in Cutchogue, 1988
25. Near Quogue, 1988
26. Just off Meadow Lane in Southampton, 1988
27. Shelter Island, 1987
28. Southampton, 1988
29. At Shinnecock Inlet County Park East, 1988
30. Historic East Hampton, 1988
31. A front yard in Roslyn Heights, 1988
32. Parrish Art Museum, 1988
33. A Sag Harbor doorstep, 1988
34. Outside the hall at Springs, 1988
35. Along Gerard Drive in East Hampton Township, 1988
36. Southampton Beach, 1988
37. Near Sands Point Preserve, 1988
38. Sag Harbor, 1988
39. Along the Montauk Highway, 1988
40. Shelter Island, 1987
41. Parrish Art Museum Courtyard, 1988
42. Along the Montauk Highway, 1988
43. Centre Island, 1988
44. Just outside Springs, 1988
45. On the South Shore, 1988
46. Looking toward the Shinnecock Inlet, 1988
47. Off the main road in Amagansett, 1988
48. West Hampton Beach, 1987

ACKNOWLEDGMENTS

My sincere thanks to the many Long Islanders who willingly stopped what they were doing to give directions, point out various landmarks, and share their feelings about why this place is so special to them. They helped me see beyond the obvious to the quiet streets, abundant fields, and expanses of sea, sky, and shore that take visitors by surprise and quickly dispel the notion that Long Island is an overcrowded extension of Manhattan.

Thanks also to the following people, who offered friendship, encouragement, and advice: John and Judy Betts, Pamela Dorman, Kimberly Gress, Terry Sears, and Susan Schulman.

LARRY KANFER is a fine art photographer with studios in Champaign and Normal, Illinois. He was born in St. Louis, Missouri, in 1956, but spent much of his boyhood in the Pacific Northwest. He graduated from the University of Illinois at Urbana-Champaign with a degree in architectural studies. Kanfer is also the author of *Prairiescapes* (University of Illinois Press, 1987). He has received several awards of excellence for his interpretive landscape photography, which has been exhibited widely in New York and throughout the country.